To all the wonderful weirdos of the world —Z.A.

Thank you to the friends, bandmates, teachers, and students who taught me it's okay to be different —K.Y.

Text copyright © 2025 by Zaila Avant-garde
Jacket art and interior illustrations copyright © 2025 by Kah Yangni

All rights reserved. Published in the United States by Doubleday, an imprint of Random House Children's Books, a division of Penguin Random House LLC, 1745 Broadway, New York, NY 10019.

DOUBLEDAY YR with colophon is a registered trademark of Penguin Random House LLC.

Visit us on the Web! rhcbooks.com

Educators and librarians, for a variety of teaching tools, visit us at RHTeachersLibrarians.com

Library of Congress Cataloging-in-Publication Data
Names: Avant-garde, Zaila, author. | Yangni, Kah, illustrator.
Title: Weird and wonderful you / by Zaila Avant-garde ; illustrated by Kah Yangni.
Description: First edition. | New York : Doubleday, 2025. | Audience: Ages 3–7. | Summary: Nonconforming individuals celebrate their unique interests and embrace what makes them wonderfully weird.
Identifiers: LCCN 2024031237 (print) | LCCN 2024031238 (ebook) | ISBN 978-0-593-56896-5 (trade) | ISBN 978-0-593-56897-2 (lib. bdg.) | ISBN 978-0-593-56898-9 (ebook)
Subjects: CYAC: Individual differences—Fiction. | LCGFT: Picture books.
Classification: LCC PZ7.1.A97326 We 2025 (print) | LCC PZ7.1.A97326 (ebook) | DDC [E]—dc23

MANUFACTURED IN CHINA
10 9 8 7 6 5 4 3 2 1

First Edition

Random House Children's Books supports the First Amendment and celebrates the right to read.

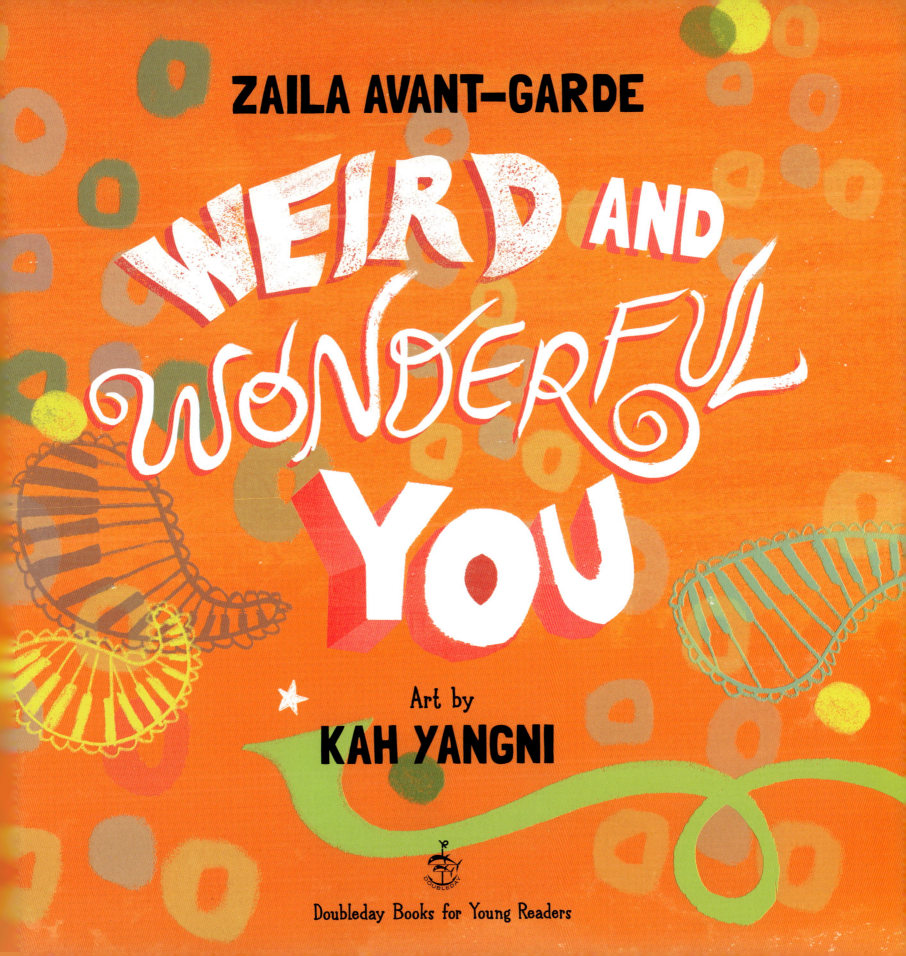

We are perfectly weird and weirdly perfect.

We are 100 percent ourselves.

"Your self-worth is determined by you. You don't have to depend on someone telling you who you are." —Beyoncé

To the ones who get called weird, CONGRATULATIONS!

"It's hard to be a diamond in a rhinestone world."
—Dolly Parton

I am winning at being weird.

I'm obsessed with the smell the earth makes when it rains. (Nerd note: it's called petrichor.)

I love cool math tricks and how frilled-neck lizards run.

Huge, sparkly butterfly wings? Wear them! Take up all the space you want.

"Never be limited by other people's limited imaginations."
—Dr. Mae Jemison

We bloom in the wild.

We are a field of pink and purple dandelions.

We are the uncontrollable weeds in your front yard.

We are a wild and gnarly tree with branches twisting every which way, up, up, into the sky.

"There is a crack in everything. That's how the light gets in."
—Leonard Cohen

"During our brief stay on planet Earth, we owe ourselves and our descendants the opportunity to explore."
—Neil deGrasse Tyson

"You change the world by being yourself."
—Yoko Ono

Stay weird,
stay wild,
stay wonderful . . .